BIGFOOT

The Legend Lives On

by L. L. Owens

Perfection Learning®

Cover & Inside Illustration: Mike Aspengren
Designer: Jan M. Michalson

About the Author

Lisa L. Owens grew up in the Midwest. She studied English and journalism at the University of Iowa. She has been a reporter, a proofreader, and an editor.

Other books by Ms. Owens include *The Spirit of the Wild West* and *Eye on Ancient Egypt*. Ms. Owens now lives near Seattle with her husband, Timothy Johnson.

Acknowledgments

Thanks to Grover Krantz for sharing his unique perspective.

Thanks to Greg Long for graciously sharing his reporting experiences—and for providing Web researchers with a valuable site.

Note

The characters, specific campsites, and other elements that move the story are purely fictional.

Art and Photo Credits

Image Credits: Art Today pp. 5, 7, 8, 10, 13, 14, 16, 19, 21, 23, 26, 31–33, 38, 50; National Archives p. 43; Corel Professional Photos pp. 6, 9; Rene Dahinden pp. 11, 18.

Table of Contents

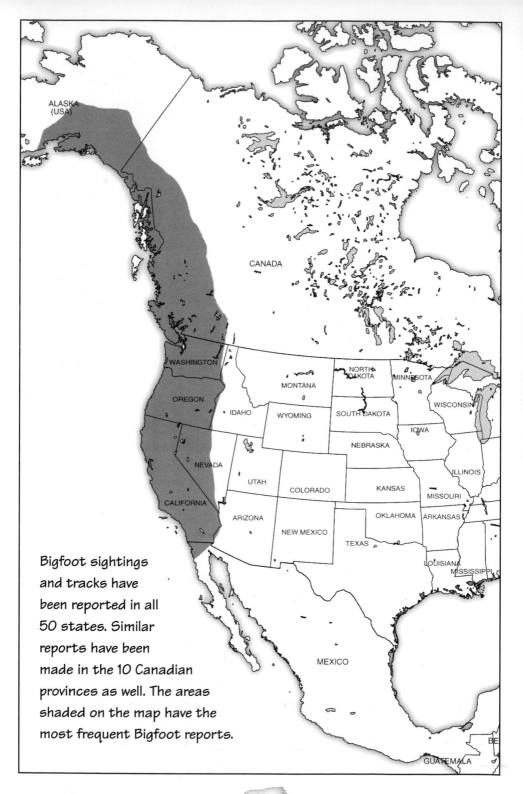

Bigfoot sightings and tracks have been reported in all 50 states. Similar reports have been made in the 10 Canadian provinces as well. The areas shaded on the map have the most frequent Bigfoot reports.

A Legendary Figure

The **legend** of Bigfoot is alive and well all over the world. The mere mention of Bigfoot—or Yeti—or Sasquatch—brings to mind a scary creature. Most legends describe him as a giant, hairy beast. And so do most people who claim to have seen him.

In the U.S. alone, thousands of people have made such claims. The largest number of Bigfoot sightings have been in the thick forests of the Pacific Northwest.

The earliest sighting on record dates back to 1000 A.D. That's when Norwegian explorer Leif Eriksson first visited the New World. Eriksson wrote that he'd seen monsters. He said they were "horribly ugly, hairy, and swarthy—and with great black eyes."

But Bigfoot legends existed in North America long before Eriksson arrived. Native Americans had been passing down such tales for generations.

This story takes place in and around Mount Rainier National Park. Read along as 11-year-old Ben Davis tries to unravel the Bigfoot mystery. He learns about Bigfoot in the news. He gains firsthand experience with Bigfoot **hoaxes.** And he meets a Yakama Indian, who discusses Bigfoot's place in cultural mythology.

Chapter 1

Welcome to Bigfoot Country

The hunter green minivan rolled to a stop. Jack and Brooke Davis had been driving all day. Their two children, Benjamin and Jessica, were asleep in the back.

"Mount Rainier National Park," sighed Brooke. "I can't believe we're actually here. What a gorgeous part of the country."

Eleven-year-old Ben's eyes flew open. He flung open his door. And he leapt to the ground.

"Finally!" Ben exclaimed. "I thought we'd never get here." He tapped on Jess's window. "Care to join us, Sleeping Beauty?"

Jess stretched and rubbed her eyes. "Where are we, Dad?" she asked.

"We're at the Trading Post General Store," replied Jack. "Just outside the campgrounds. We thought we'd fill the cooler and go set up camp."

Ben rapped on his sister's window again. "Hey!" he cried. "Last one inside pitches the tent alone!" Then he sprinted toward the store. He glanced behind him. Sure enough, Jessica was scrambling to catch up. She couldn't stand to be left behind. And Ben knew it. He stopped and put one foot inside the store. He blocked Jess's way with the other.

"I beat you," he teased.

"No fair!" Jess shouted. "You called it before I was even out of my seatbelt!"

"Sorry, Jess. You snooze, you lose!"

"Mom! Do I have to pitch the tent by myself?"

"Of course not, honey," Brooke answered. "We *all* help. Right, Jack?"

"Right," nodded Jack. "You kids go on in and pick out a snack. We'll be right there. I'm going to fill up the gas tank. And your mom's going to evaluate the food situation."

The kids burst into the store.

"It's almost closing time, kids," said Mr. Cooper. He owned the Trading Post. "What'll it be?"

"I'm dying for a soda," said Ben.

"Mmmm—that sounds good," added Jess.

"She always wants what I want," Ben told Mr. Cooper.

"I bet she does. I'll get a couple from the back. Just make yourselves at home. Have a look around."

Ben scanned the room. The store was on the bottom floor of a two-story log cabin. The walls were covered with **memorabilia.** There were hunting tools. Mounted fish. Old-time lanterns and other camping gear. And many Native American **artifacts.**

Ben shook his head in disbelief. "Look at all this stuff," he said.

Then Jack and Brooke walked inside.

"These kids with you?" asked Mr. Cooper.

"Yes," said Brooke. "We're Jack and Brooke Davis. I see you've met Ben and Jess."

"Pleased to meet you. I'm Sam Cooper. Are you camping nearby? Or just passing through?"

"We're camping at the Big Firs site for a few days. So you'll probably see quite a bit of us."

"Let me know if I can help—with anything. I know the mountain and the trails. And I try to keep the store well-stocked. Mostly with everything people tend to leave at home. Like food, first-aid kits, paperbacks, toothpaste, live bait, camping supplies. You name it. If I don't have it, I can probably get it."

"That's great to know," said Jack. "I think we came prepared. But it's nice to have the store so close."

"Have you kids been camping before?" asked Mr. Cooper.

"Yes," said Ben. "But we've never been so far up in the mountains. We're going to do some hiking."

"And swimming," added Jack. "And canoeing. And bird-watching."

"You've certainly picked the right place to do all that," said Mr. Cooper. "I hope you brought your camera. You'll want to capture all the incredible **flora** and **fauna.**"

"What's that?" asked Jess.

"He means the plants and the wildlife," replied Brooke.

The Flora and Fauna of Mount Rainier

The environment on Mount Rainier is varied. Different **elevations** produce different **climates.** So different plants and animals **inhabit** the land at different elevations.

The forests of Mount Rainier National Park make up 60 percent of the park's landscape. There are evergreen, fir, cedar, and hemlock trees.

Flowers in the lowland forest bloom from late April through late June.

In July and August, more than 30 different flowers bloom in the **subalpine** meadows. The colorful meadows are popular tourist attractions.

People began stocking the park's lakes with fish in the early 1900s. This practice was stopped in 1972. Salmon are believed to have always lived in the park's waters. Bull trout also live there.

The mammals of Mount Rainier live in the climate that best suits them. Occasionally, animals travel from zone to zone in search of food. These are the mammals that live on the mountain.

Beaver	Mountain goat
Black bear	Mountain lion
Black-tailed deer	Northern flying squirrel
Bobcat	Pika
Coyote	Pine marten
Douglas pine squirrel	Porcupine
Elk	Raccoon
Golden mantled ground squirrel	Snowshoe hare
Hoary marmot	Yellow pine chipmunk

Source: National Park Service

"Man, I can't wait to see the wild animals!" exclaimed Ben. "I plan to do a little exploring. I promised my friends that I'd bring back pictures. I want to get a bear and a mountain lion and a coyote—"

"Whoa there, Ben," said Brooke. "We talked about this. We're sticking to the park's public trails. We probably won't even see those animals up close. At least I hope not."

"You're such a worrywart, Mom. We *are* out in the wilderness, you know. So we're bound to see something. Isn't that right, Mr. Cooper?"

"You're right, Ben. You are bound to see *something.*" Mr. Cooper paused. He had a playful twinkle in his eye. "But you may not always know exactly what you're looking at."

Other Names for Bigfoot

Abominable Snowman
Alma
Big Elder Brother
Chinese Wildman
Hairy Ghost
Minnesota Iceman
One Who Runs and Hides
Sasquatch
Stick Shower Indian
Stone Giant
Timber Giant
Upslope Person
Wicked Cannibal Giant
Wood Man
Yeti
Yowie

"What do you mean?" asked Jess.

"Well, Jess, you see . . . no . . . I'd better not. It might scare you." Mr. Cooper closed his mouth. Then he pretended to lock up his lips and throw away the key.

"Oh, please, Mr. Cooper!" exclaimed Jess. "You have to tell us now!"

Mr. Cooper laughed. "Okay. Let's see—what was I saying again?"

"You were about to tell us about the wild animals we might see," prompted Ben.

"Did I say 'wild *animals'?*" asked Mr. Cooper. "Funny, I don't remember using that term."

"You're not saying there are wild *people* out there," said Ben.

"No. Not exactly. Have you ever heard of Sasquatch?"

"Oh—I almost forgot," laughed Jack. "We're in Bigfoot country, kids."

"That's right," replied Mr. Cooper. "You're right in the heart of it."

"But Bigfoot's just a myth," chuckled Ben. "He doesn't really exist."

"Doesn't he?" teased Mr. Cooper. "You seem pretty sure of that, son. Especially for someone who's never been this far up in the mountains."

Mr. Cooper pointed to a glass case. Inside was a plaster cast. It looked like a giant foot. "What do you make of that?" he asked.

Ben and the others examined it. A sign next to it read, "Cast of a genuine Bigfoot footprint. The footprint was found by a group of hikers on the Golden Gate Trail. August 8, 1994."

"Wow!" exclaimed Ben. "So you've met Bigfoot?"

"No, I haven't," said Mr. Cooper. "But I did meet the folks who had the sighting. They gave me this cast."

"What do you think, Dad?" asked Jess.

"I think that's something else," he answered, putting his hand on her shoulder. "And I think we'd better get moving. We've got to set up camp. And Mr. Cooper's got to close his store."

"But I want to hear more about Bigfoot," said Ben.

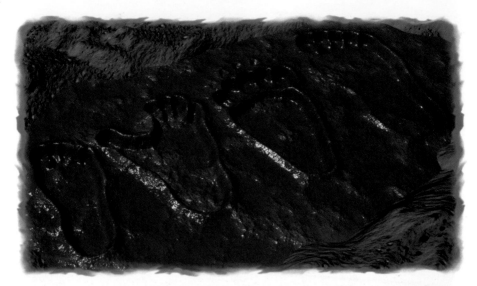

"You should do as your dad says," said Mr. Cooper. "Come by tomorrow. I'll tell you some stories."

"Thanks, Sam," said Brooke. "I'm sure we'll see you again." Then she laughed, "In the meantime, we'll be sure to watch out for a scary, hairy beast."

As Brooke spoke, an older man entered the store. His silver hair was in long braids. He politely nodded to Brooke. Then he said, "Hi, Sam. I see you're showing off your footprint again." Then, turning to the others, he said, "Hope you folks aren't too **gullible!"**

"Have *you* seen Bigfoot?" Ben asked eagerly.

"Ben!" said Jack. "You haven't even introduced yourself."

"I'm sorry, sir," said Ben. "I'm Ben Davis. This is my younger sister Jess. And these are my parents."

"We're Brooke and Jack," said Brooke.

"Glad to know you. I'm Jim. Sam and I play chess every Monday night. And—no—I haven't seen Bigfoot." He winked at Ben.

"Hope to see you around," said Jack. "And now we really do need to get going." To the kids, he added, "Who wants hot dogs over the campfire?"

"I do!" shouted Jess. "Can we toast marshmallows later?"

"It wouldn't be camping without 'em," smiled Brooke.

"Good-bye, folks," Mr. Cooper said.

With a wave, Ben said, "See you tomorrow." And the family left the store.

Mr. Cooper rubbed his hands together and grinned. He said to Jim, "Looks like I've got a new victim!"

"Do you mean the boy? He's young, Sam," Jim cautioned. "Go easy on him."

"I will," promised Mr. Cooper. "But you have to admit—boys his age love to be scared out of their wits. Besides, he's obviously a smart kid. He'll figure it out."

"I hope so," Jim laughed. "Now—let's play chess!"

Chapter 2

Caution! Big, Hairy Creature—Straight Ahead!

Ben awoke at the crack of dawn. The family was going canoeing. So he was eager to get started. Plus, the sooner he got back, the sooner he could visit Mr. Cooper. And he could learn that much more about Bigfoot!

Over blueberry pancakes, Ben asked, "How far are we going to canoe this morning?"

"Oh, about ten miles," Brooke replied.

"How long will that take?"

"I'm not sure."

"Well, what time do you think we'll get back?"

"Why?" asked Jack. "Do you have other plans?"

"You know I want to talk to Mr. Cooper, Dad."

"Yes, I know," he laughed. "It's the only thing you talked about last night."

"Don't worry," said Brooke. "We'll be back early this afternoon. That should give you plenty of time to visit Mr. Cooper."

"Great!" said Ben. He couldn't wait.

"Speaking of canoeing," said Jack. "We'd better clean up this mess. We're scheduled to meet our guide in half an hour. Her name is Cindy. She'll be at the Visitor Center."

It was a perfect morning. The sky was clear and crystal blue. The lush, green land along the Carbon River was breathtaking. Cindy pointed out the different flowers, plants, and animals. And she taught everyone how to row the canoe.

Ben was having a good time. Until—suddenly—he spotted a huge black creature. It was wading in the water up ahead. But it wasn't close enough for him to make out.

"What's that?" shouted Ben. He felt a strange sense of alarm.

Cindy said, "It's a black bear. He's probably looking for fish."

"Are you sure?" asked Ben. "It looks more like a—maybe a gorilla—or *something.*"

"I'm sure," said Cindy. She pulled out her binoculars. "Here. Take a look."

Ben peered through the binoculars. He focused. Then he sighed, "It's a bear, all right."

"What else would it be, silly?" asked Jess.

"Nothing," answered Ben. "It's a bear. I can see that it's a bear."

"You sound disappointed, son," said Jack. "I figured you'd want to snap some pictures of him."

"Sure I do, Dad. I'll get some when we go by."

"I get it!" Jess sang out. "Ben thought the bear was Bigfoot!"

"I did not!" Ben snapped. "I just couldn't tell what it was at first. That's all."

Cindy said, "If you want pictures, you'd better start snapping. Looks like our friend is leaving."

Ben quickly took a few shots. And the bear disappeared into the woods. "Darn," he said. "Those will probably be kind of fuzzy. I didn't hold the camera very steady. And I only got him from behind."

"I have an idea," said Jess. "The bear was standing on his hind legs for a couple of those. Right?"

"Yeah. So?"

"I bet you could try to pass them off as photos of Bigfoot!" Jess giggled. "Who's gonna know?"

"Cut it out, Jess!" Ben demanded.

"Your sister's got a point there, Ben," chuckled Cindy. "You'd be surprised at how many people claim that their bear pictures are really Bigfoot."

"Why would they do that?" asked Ben.

"Well, some people like to play a joke. Or get on the news," she said. "Others really believe that they've seen Bigfoot. But there's

Unlike Patterson's film, experts say this photo is a hoax.

usually some expert who can prove the creature was a bear—or something else."

Cindy continued. "Then you have people like Roger Patterson. He filmed what he believed was Bigfoot. This was a long time ago. Experts from all over have looked at the film. And nobody has ever been able to prove that it was fake. Or that the creature in it wasn't Bigfoot. It's something to think about, anyway."

The Patterson Film

October 20, 1967, was an important day. At least it was for Roger Patterson and Bob Gimlin. That's the day they claimed to have seen—and filmed—Bigfoot.

Patterson had been fascinated with Bigfoot for years. When he set out to find Bigfoot in Bluff Creek, California, Gimlin went along.

According to Patterson, they searched for seven days. They found nothing. On the eighth day, they were riding their horses near a stream. Suddenly, they saw what they thought was Bigfoot.

Patterson's horse was frightened. And Patterson fell to the ground.

According to both men, the creature paused. It stared back at them. Gimlin aimed his rifle—just in case. The animal fled. And Patterson turned on his movie camera. He'd been filming scenery all day. So after just 53 seconds, he ran out of film.

Many scientists say the Patterson film is a hoax. Others, however, feel that it is real.

In any case, the **authenticity** of the film has never been disproved.

18

"Wow!" Ben exclaimed. "What do you think?"

Cindy replied, "I think that you have to weigh all the evidence. So many people have claimed to see Bigfoot over the years. Who knows? We do have the perfect environment out here.

"Then again, there was this man a few years back. He confessed to leaving fake Bigfoot footprints around. He said he'd been doing it for a long time—just for fun!"

Fake Tracks

In 1982, 86-year-old Rant Mullens admitted to regularly faking Bigfoot tracks. He said that he'd been leaving huge footprints all over the Pacific Northwest. (For over 50 years!) And he told investigators which "sightings" had been the result of his pranks.

He said that he had carved "Bigfoot feet" from wood. He wore them like shoes. Then he made tracks in mud, snow, and so on.

Interestingly, the authorities didn't believe Mullens' story. They said he wasn't heavy enough to have made the deep, three-dimensional tracks they'd found.

According to *Hoaxes!* by Gordon Stein and Marie J. MacNee, so-called Bigfoot experts didn't believe Mullens either. Several of them swore that they could tell the difference between a real Bigfoot track and a track made from a big wooden shoe.

"So it's all make-believe!" exclaimed Ben. "I knew it!"

"I didn't say that," replied Cindy. "A lot of people—even some scientists—take Bigfoot very seriously. For example, Professor Grover Krantz—he lives right here in Washington. He wrote a book about Bigfoot. He thinks that Bigfoot may be a species of **Gigantopithecus.** And he cautions people to keep an open mind."

An Interview with Professor Grover Krantz

Grover Krantz is a professor of anthropology at Washington State University. His main area of study is human evolution. And he is an authority on *cryptozoology,* or the study of hidden animals. He has been widely interviewed on the topic of Bigfoot. And he wrote the 1992 book *Big Footprints: A Scientific Inquiry into the Reality of Sasquatch.*

Question: Why are you interested in Bigfoot?

Answer: I have a curiosity about things that are unusual or unexplained. (But not a belief in them.) And I believe that science should be involved in trying to solve such problems. Also, Bigfoot is related to my field of work.

Question: Do you believe Bigfoot exists?

Answer: I've seen masses of **data** on sightings and footprints that suggest the existence of the creature. If Bigfoot does not exist, then ALL of these hundreds of cases must be otherwise explained. It is harder to believe that he doesn't exist.

Question: Do "hoax" sightings damage the **credibility** of serious research?

Answer: Hoaxes damage the investigation only to the degree that they are publicized. Weekly **tabloids** are the worst offenders.

Question: Have you ever had a sighting?

Answer: I have not.

Question: You've compared modern doubt about the existence of sasquatches to 17th- and 18th-century doubt about the gorilla's existence. True?

Answer: The gorilla's existence was proven by finding the remains of one for scientific study. Only the same will settle the Bigfoot problem.

Question: What advice would you give to kids who might want to investigate Bigfoot as adults?

Answer: Get some expertise in hunting and tracking. And be the one who brings in the first **specimen.** Otherwise, get training in a technical field that relates to the investigation. (Such as zoology, anthropology, forestry, etc.) Look for more evidence through your work.

After canoeing, the Davises drove into a nearby town. They ate lunch and browsed through some shops. Then they headed back to their campsite.

"I could really go for a nap," yawned Jack.

"No way," said Brooke. "We're not wasting our time here by sleeping during the day."

"But we never get to take naps at home," complained Jack. "Aren't we supposed to relax on vacation?"

Brooke rolled her eyes. "There's a nice pool at the other end of the campgrounds. Who wants to go for a swim?"

Jess jumped up and down. "I do, I do!" she cried.

"Okay, I'll go too," said Jack. "That'll perk me up. Ben? What about you?"

"I'd rather visit Mr. Cooper, Dad," admitted Ben. "If that's okay with you."

"It's fine, honey," said Brooke. "I'm sure Mr. Cooper's invitation was sincere. But he is working. So promise to stay out of his way. Especially when he has customers. Deal?"

"Deal!" declared Ben. And with that, he sprinted off to the Trading Post.

Jack called after him. "Don't go anywhere else without checking with us! And be back in time for dinner!"

"Got it!" Ben yelled over his shoulder.

Chapter 3

Ben Searches for Answers

Ben hurried into the store. Mr. Cooper was behind the counter.

"Hello, Ben," said Mr. Cooper. "Where's the rest of your family?"

"They're swimming. I figure I can do that back home. Do you have time to talk today?"

"I think so," answered Mr. Cooper. "It's usually slow around here in the early afternoon. What would you like to hear about?"

"Everything!" proclaimed Ben. "Anything you know about Bigfoot, that is."

Mr. Cooper threw back his head and laughed. "I see you've worked up quite a curiosity!" he said. "I'll tell you what I know. But I'm no expert. I just collect information as a hobby. The tourists like to hear about it."

Mr. Cooper took an overstuffed scrapbook from a cabinet. He showed Ben some drawings and photos. There were lots of news clippings too.

Ben read one clipping with interest.

The Wild Men of California

This is an abridged version of a letter written to a California newspaper. It appeared in the Port Hope Guide *on November 18, 1870.*

I saw in your paper an item concerning the gorilla seen in Crow Cannon. You sneered at the idea of there being any such critters in these hills.

I positively assure you that this gorilla, or wild man, or whatever you choose to call it is no myth. I know it exists and that there are at least two of them.

Last fall, I was hunting in the mountains 20 miles south of here. I camped five or six times in one place. Several times, I returned to my camp after a hunt. I saw that the ashes and charred sticks from the fireplace had been scattered about. An old hunter notices such things and very soon gets curious to know the cause.

My bedding and traps were not disturbed. But I was anxious to learn who or what was so regularly visiting my camp. I saw no tracks near the camp. About 300 yards off, in damp sand, I struck the track of a man's feet— I supposed. It was bare and of immense size.

I took a position on a hillside about 60 or 70 feet from the fire. I hid in the brush. I waited and watched.

The fireplace was on my right. The spot where I saw the track was on my left. It was in this direction that my attention was mostly directed.

Suddenly, I was startled by a shrill whistle. I turned quickly. I exclaimed as I saw the creature standing beside my fire, looking suspiciously around. It was in the image of a man. But it could not have been human. I was never so astonished before.

The creature, whatever it was, stood five feet high. It was broad and square at the shoulders with arms of great length. The legs were short and the body long. The head was small compared with the rest of the creature. It appeared to be set upon his shoulders without a neck. It was covered with dark brown and cinnamon-colored hair—quite long on some parts.

As I looked, he threw his head back and whistled again. Then he stooped and grasped a stick from the fire. This he swung around and around until the fire on the end had gone out. Then he repeated the maneuver. I was dumb almost and could only look. Fifteen minutes I sat and watched as he whistled and scattered my fire about.

I could have easily put a bullet through his head. But why should I kill him?

He started to go. Having gone a short distance, he returned and was joined by another—a female. They both turned and walked past me—within 20 yards of where I sat. They disappeared into the brush. I could not have had a better opportunity for observing them.

I have told this story many times since then. It has often raised a skeptical smile. But I have met one person who has seen those mysterious creatures. And I've met a dozen who have come across their tracks.

"That's a pretty good story," said Ben. "Do you think it's true?"

"It's hard to say. Stories like that have been told for years and years. The remarkable thing to me, though, is how similar they are."

"Maybe people read about Bigfoot," guessed Ben. "Then they make their story fit the details."

"Could be," said Mr. Cooper. "But that would take a lot of research. Especially if someone wanted to purposely fit a tale to the details of all the others."

"That's a good point," said Ben. "I wish I knew what to believe."

"You should believe whatever you feel comfortable believing."

"What do you believe, Mr. Cooper?"

"That's strictly between me—and me," smiled Mr. Cooper. "You can make up your own mind."

Ben said, "Hearing more would help. What can you tell me?"

"I can tell you some of the basics. Like the details of Bigfoot's appearance. And how he acts."

"I'd love to hear all that," said Ben eagerly.

"First of all," began Mr. Cooper, "Bigfoot is about seven or eight feet tall. He weighs about 800 pounds. He is covered with dark brown fur. And he walks upright with a slight slouch. His footprints are about 18–24 inches long. And they're up to 8 inches wide.

"Some say that he gives off a very strong, **offensive** odor. He makes a high-pitched whistling noise. In fact, I've heard strange noises many times. It sounds like a birdcall. It can be pretty spooky."

"He sounds scary," said Ben. "I don't think I want to meet him."

"You don't necessarily have to worry about that," said Mr. Cooper. "Not if you don't *really* believe in him."

"I don't understand," said Ben.

Mr. Cooper looked around the store. There was nobody there. He turned back to Ben. He leaned down. Then he spoke in a low voice—

"According to some legends, Bigfoot appears *only* to people who believe in him. So if you don't believe, you just might be safe."

"What would happen if, say, someone like me saw him?" asked Ben. "Would he hurt me?"

"Probably not. *If* you didn't threaten him. That's what most people say. And if you saw his footprints, or some other sign, it would be better to ignore them."

"Why?"

"It's best not to take any chances," Mr. Cooper said seriously. "He could be hiding—and watching. If he sees you poking around his tracks, he might feel threatened. Who knows? Maybe he'd follow you. Or worse!"

Mr. Cooper straightened up. "It looks like I've said too much," he said, studying Ben's face. "I hope I haven't frightened you."

"Oh, no! Of course not!" Ben lied.

"Well, I do suppose that's enough Bigfoot talk for one day."

Ben looked at his watch. He'd been talking with Mr. Cooper for hours. "I'd better get back to the campsite," he said. "We're having a fish fry tonight."

"Sounds good," said Mr. Cooper. Then he chuckled and poked Ben in the ribs. "Hope no unwanted visitors show up."

"Me too," said Ben. And he meant it!

"What are you doing tomorrow?"

"Mom has big plans. We're going to hike on Mount Rainier."

Mr. Cooper looked interested. "Which trail?" he said.

"I think it's called the Golden Gate Trail."

"You're kidding!" Mr. Cooper exclaimed. "That's where that Bigfoot sighting was in '94!"

"Really?" Ben asked. He tried to hide his excitement. "I remember now. That's where your footprint came from."

"Yes, it is. You never know . . . you might see something yourself. Wouldn't that be exciting?" Mr. Cooper sighed. Then he said, "What am I saying! A clever boy like you—you probably think all this talk is a bunch of hogwash."

"No, I don't," said Ben. "I still don't know what to think."

"Well, I wouldn't worry about it. I'm sure you won't see anything. If you do, though, remember what I said. Ignore it. Better safe than sorry, I always say."

"Right," said Ben. "I'll ignore all signs of Bigfoot!" And he gave a brave laugh. Just in case Mr. Cooper was joking.

"Attaboy!" replied Mr. Cooper. "Have a good time. And keep your guard up."

"I will," Ben said. As he walked back, he vowed, "Bigfoot will never get me."

Chapter 4

Things That Go "THUD" in the Night

It was late at night. All the Davises were asleep. Except Ben. He tossed and turned in his sleeping bag. He was trying to decide—once and for all—what he believed.

Bigfoot can't be real, he thought. Someone would have captured him by now.

He struggled to put Bigfoot out of his mind. But he couldn't. Every time he closed his eyes, he saw Bigfoot looming over him.

I've got to stop thinking about this! he thought. If I don't, he's liable to become real. And he'll pay me a visit! I don't believe. I don't believe. I don't believe. I don't believe.

Suddenly, the midnight silence was broken. Ben heard a high screeching sound in the distance.

"It's just a bird," Ben whispered. "Nothing to be afraid of."

But he wasn't entirely convinced. He had listened to tapes of birdcalls at the ranger station. And none of them had sounded like that.

They couldn't have *every* bird on tape, Ben thought. He heard the screech again. This time, it sounded closer! Then—

THUD. THUD. THUD. THUD.

What's that noise? Ben thought. It sounds like heavy footsteps!

THUD. THUD. THUD. THUD.

A massive shadow appeared over the top of the tent. Right over Ben's sleeping bag!

Is that a bear? Ben thought. Or is it—no! I can't think that!

He was beginning to panic a little. He heard a popping sound. (Perhaps it was a stick breaking.) Then he caught a whiff of a horrible odor.

"Ugh!" Ben coughed.

Then Jack awoke with a start. "What's wrong, Ben?" he asked.

"That smell—I think it's—"

"Must be a skunk," Jack said. "It'll pass soon. Try to go back to sleep."

"I will, Dad," said Ben. "Sorry I woke you." He was glad that he hadn't finished his sentence. He had been about to say that it smelled like Bigfoot!

Jack fell back to sleep in seconds. And Ben was alone again. At least it seemed that way to him.

"Okay," he whispered to himself. "Get a hold of yourself. Enough is enough. Those noises could have been made by any animal. That shadow was probably just a tree branch, bending in the breeze. And Dad's right. I bet a skunk got spooked and left its scent. Everything can be explained. There's nothing strange going on here. Nothing to be afraid of . . ."

Ben clutched his sleeping bag. And he listened to the night.

5

Footprints and Fur

Brooke gave Ben a gentle shake. "Time to get up, honey," she said.

Ben woke from a fitful sleep. His grip on his sleeping bag was still tight. Slowly, he focused on his mom. "What time is it?" he asked.

"It's 6:00," she replied. "We start the hike in one hour. Come on out for your dad's famous power breakfast. He's got granola with strawberries and bananas. And freshly squeezed orange juice."

Ben dressed and joined the others. He ate quietly. He was still trying to make sense of the night before.

Did I imagine all those things? he wondered.

By the light of day, that seemed likely.

Brooke interrupted Ben's thoughts. "Ben, when you're ready, we all need to review the hiking tips. Cindy gave them to me yesterday."

Ben hurried off to brush his teeth. When he came back, Brooke outlined the park's rules.

Hiking Safety Tips

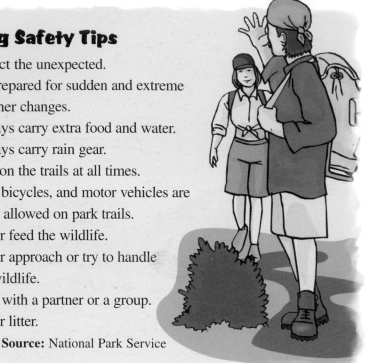

1. Expect the unexpected.
2. Be prepared for sudden and extreme weather changes.
3. Always carry extra food and water.
4. Always carry rain gear.
5. Stay on the trails at all times.
6. Pets, bicycles, and motor vehicles are NOT allowed on park trails.
7. Never feed the wildlife.
8. Never approach or try to handle the wildlife.
9. Hike with a partner or a group.
10. Never litter.

Source: National Park Service

At 7:00 A.M. sharp, the Davises met Cindy at the Visitor Center.

"Hello, troops," she said cheerfully. "Who's ready to hike?"

"I'm as ready as I'll ever be," smiled Jack.

"Then let's go!" she exclaimed.

As they hiked, Cindy told them about the park and its trails. "About 2 million people hike these trails each year," she said. "There are 300+ miles of them."

"When does the snow melt up here?" asked Jess.

"The snow on the trails usually melts by mid-July. But then it comes down again starting in October."

Meanwhile, Ben kept an eye out for suspicious-looking creatures. "Hey, Jess," he said at one point. "Look over there. Do you see the deer?"

"Oh, they're beautiful!" she said. "Cindy, can I give the little ones some trail mix?"

"Absolutely not," Cindy answered firmly. "Sorry, Jess. But it's against the park's policy for visitors to feed the animals."

"Will the food hurt them?" asked Brooke.

"Yes," Cindy replied. "In several ways. You see, the fawns would love to eat the trail mix. But it would not be good for them.

"And if they are fed by humans too many times, they will start to expect it. Then they won't search for their natural food."

"I can see how that would be a problem," said Brooke.

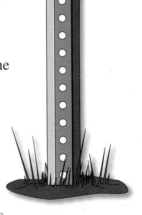

Caution!

The animals are beautiful. But please enjoy them from a safe distance. No feeding or handling allowed. Remember, feeding the animals attracts them to places in unnatural numbers. And that can lead to disease and starvation.

At lunchtime, the group stopped at a small clearing. Just as they had planned. Ben rushed to finish his peanut butter and jelly sandwich.

"Dad?" he asked. "May I be excused?"

"Don't you want to rest?" said Jack. "We're only halfway done."

"I'm not tired. I just want to look at the fork in the trail. The part that goes west. I won't go far."

"Okay," said Jack. "But stay where I can see you. And take your apple."

"Thanks!"

With that, Ben tramped over to the fork in the trail. He saw the big rock he was looking for. He'd seen it in a photo at the Trading Post.

"Here it is," he said to himself. "People saw Bigfoot right here."

The rock was on the trail itself. It stood taller than Ben. He walked behind it. Branches from the woods hung over the small open space like a ceiling. It created a rather dark, damp **haven.** And Ben realized he was hidden from view.

What a great fort this would make! he thought.

He began searching for fresh evidence. "It's like Mr. Cooper said," he murmured. "You never know."

Then something caught his eye. It was a large stick. Ben took a closer look. The stick had a tuft of brownish black hair on it.

Next he circled the rock. He noticed tracks in the mud—two enormous tracks! They were shaped like human footprints. But they were at least 20 inches long. It looked like they had emerged from the grass just beyond the rock.

Ben's head was spinning. Without thinking, he snapped a couple of pictures.

"Bigfoot was here!" he said. "Maybe he's still nearby. I'd better tell Dad. But—wait—I can't! Mr. Cooper said that might cause trouble. Okay, then. I'll walk away. I'll pretend I didn't see this."

Ben rushed back to the others. He didn't dare say anything.

Brooke noticed that he was out of breath. "Everything okay,

Ben?" She felt his forehead.

"I'm fine, Mom," Ben answered.

"Are you sure? You look a little flushed. And your brow is sweaty."

"I said I was fine," he asserted.

"He's just hot from chasing after Bigfoot," Jess teased.

"You don't know what you're talking about!" Ben snapped.

"Hey, son, relax," said Jack. "Jess was just kidding."

Ben apologized. "Sorry. I didn't mean to bite your head off. I'm just eager to finish the hike."

"Apology accepted," said Jess. "*If* you show me how to make S'mores tonight. You promised."

"Okay."

"Hey, troops," Cindy said. "Time to get moving."

Good! Ben thought. I need to get as far away from here as I can. And fast!

Ben tried to force Bigfoot out of his mind. Again, it was no use. He definitely had Bigfoot on the brain!

He struggled with this most of the way down the trail. Then he had an idea. He decided to start singing.

I want Bigfoot to hear me, he thought. Then *he'll* think that *I'm* not thinking—or talking—about him. And he'll know that I don't believe in him!

Ben asked the group, "Who wants to sing?"

Jess did, of course. Jack and Brooke said they would. And Cindy said, "Good idea, Ben. That'll help us finish the last leg of the trail. Pick something lively. Then start us off."

Ben thought of a song he'd learned at camp last year. And he belted it out—

> "John Jacob Jingle Heimer Schmitt
> That's my name too
> Whenever I go out,
> The people always shout—
> There goes John Jacob Jingle Heimer Schmitt!
> Da-da-da-da-da-da-da—"

The others joined in right away. Everyone knew it! They repeated the same words over and over. Each verse got a little softer. Until the sixth time. They sang so softly that it was barely audible. Then—in no time—they were back where they'd started.

Back at the campsite, Ben was still uneasy. He wanted to tell Mr. Cooper about the tracks. And the fur.

"Mom?"

"Yes, Ben," she answered.

"May I go to the Trading Post?"

"Again?" Brooke asked. "Mr. Cooper might need a break."

"I won't stay long. Besides, I promised Jess that I'd make S'mores," he said. "So I need to get the stuff."

"All right," Brooke said. She fished a ten-dollar bill out of her pocket. "Here's some money—and I want the change!"

"Thanks, Mom," said Ben. "See you later." Ben headed for the store. His mind was racing.

What will Mr. Cooper have to say? he wondered.

Chapter 6

Secrets and Stories

Ben ran into Jim on the path to the store.

"Hello, son," Jim said. "Where are you headed?"

"To the Trading Post," he answered.

"Me too," said Jim. "I'll walk with you."

The pair walked in silence for a minute or two. Then Jim asked, "Are you having a good time?"

"You bet," said Ben. "This is a great place. We hiked the Golden Gate Trail earlier."

"That's a pretty one. It's part of the bigger Skyline Trail. There was a Bigfoot sighting there a few years back, you know." Jim checked Ben's face for his reaction.

"Yes, I know. Mr. Cooper told me about it."

"I'm not surprised," chuckled Jim. "He loves to tell those stories. It gets the kids all riled up."

Soon they arrived at the store. But it was closed. A sign on the door read, "Back at 4:00."

"Sam must have driven into town," Jim said. "I know where the extra key is. If you need something, I can ring it up for you. Sam won't mind."

"I do need a couple of things," said Ben. "Thanks."

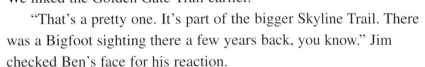

Jim took Ben into the store. And Ben gathered the ingredients for S'mores.

"Let's see," he said. "I've got graham crackers, chocolate bars, and marshmallows. I think that'll do it."

Jim rang up the sale on the cash register. "Are you heading back to camp now?" he asked.

"In a little bit," said Ben. "I was hoping to talk to Mr. Cooper."

"Well, it's 3:15 now," said Jim. "Do you want to come back later? Or would you like to wait?"

"I think I'll stick around," Ben replied. "I really don't want to miss him. He'll want to hear what I have to say."

"I see," Jim said. "Well, why don't I show you Sam's gardens in the meantime. They're out back."

"Sure," said Ben.

The pair made their way to the backyard. There were two huge gardens. One was filled with fruits and vegetables. The other was teeming with beautiful shrubs and flowers. Ben was impressed.

"He must put a lot of work into these," Ben said.

"Oh, yes," Jim nodded. "His gardens are his pride and joy. He sells much of the **produce** in the store. He grows the best tomatoes, potatoes, and cucumbers in the area. Not to mention his prize-winning blueberries and strawberries."

"Those *are* good," Ben agreed. "We've been eating his berries for breakfast."

Ben admired the gardens. But his mind was wandering. He was becoming impatient. And he wished Mr. Cooper would come back!

"So you have something important to discuss with Sam," said Jim. "Nothing's wrong, I hope. Normally, I wouldn't ask. But you seem worried."

"I saw something strange. That's all," said Ben.

"Where? On your hike?" Jim was pretty sure he knew the answer to that!

"Yes."

"Sounds interesting. Can you tell me about it?"

"I'd rather not."

Jim wondered how to handle this. Then he decided to pursue it. "Listen, Ben . . . did you happen to see this 'strange' thing at the fork in the trail?"

Ben was startled. "No!" he declared. "I didn't see anything there. Why would I?"

"Well," Jim said, "I have a feeling that you saw some Bigfoot tracks. Am I right?"

Ben could keep it in no longer. "You're right! I saw some tracks. And I saw some hair. How did you know?"

"Just a hunch, son," said Jim, laughing. "I've known Sam for a long time."

"What does Mr. Cooper have to do with it? Did he see something earlier too?"

"I'm sure he did," Jim snickered. "But he probably saw it from a different **perspective.**"

"What do you mean?"

"I mean that I'm sure he saw the tracks. But he saw them because he *made* them."

"But he couldn't have made them. They were so big."

"Let me show you something," said Jim. He led Ben to the potting shed. In the back corner were two massive shoes. They had been carved from wood. And they were shaped like feet!

Jim pointed to the still-wet mud clinging to the shoes.

"So Mr. Cooper is like that guy Cindy told us about," Ben said. "The one who used to leave fake footprints all over the Northwest."

"Sort of," Jim laughed. "Sam likes to have a little fun with the tourists."

Just then, a wave of dread washed over Ben.

"What's the matter?" Jim asked.

"I just remembered the stuff that happened last night."

"What stuff?"

"It was the middle of the night. Everyone else was sleeping. But I was awake.

"First, I heard the type of whistling sound that Bigfoot makes. I heard footsteps. I saw a huge shadow over the tent. And I smelled the most horrible smell ever. Mr. Cooper couldn't have done all that."

"Oh, but he could have," said Jim. "And I suspect that he did. He's got a whistle that makes some frightening sounds. And even an average-sized man like Sam can look huge as a shadow."

"What about the smell?"

Jim poked around the shed a little more. "A-ha!" he exclaimed. "Look at this." And he showed Ben a stink bomb! "That Sam can get his hands on anything!"

Ben was stunned. And a little angry.

"I thought Mr. Cooper was my friend," he said.

"Don't be too hard on him," Jim said. "He likes to have fun. And if I know him, he was just trying to give you a good scare. One that you'd talk about for years to come."

Jim went on. "Besides, Sam's stunts add fuel to the Bigfoot myth. And that's not altogether bad."

"Why not?" Ben asked.

"To Sam's way of thinking, Bigfoot sightings are great. They make more people talk about the area. Then maybe they'll visit. And that's good for business.

"Also, there are so many cultural myths about Bigfoot. Or Bigfoot-like creatures. Especially in the different Native American cultures. Every tribe seems to have a different Bigfoot legend. Each one serves a different purpose. And each one is part of a tribe's rich **oral tradition.**

"These stories are passed down from generation to generation. Like the one my grandfather always told me. So the legends are part of our history," Jim continued.

Yakama Indians

According to some sources, *Yakama* means "a growing family." An earlier name for the Yakamas may have been *Wap-tail-min*. This means "narrow river people." And it probably refers to the narrows in the Yakima River at Union Gap. A large village was located there long ago.

For many generations, the land of the Yakamas extended in all directions. It went from the Cascade Mountain Range to the Columbia River. The Yakamas believed that the land had been given to them by their Creator. They believed that the living were meant to use the land. And they were supposed to preserve it—and their heritage—for future generations.

Source: Yakama Nation Museum

"I love it when people become fascinated by Bigfoot. Then they want to learn more. And they often end up learning more about Native American cultures too," Jim said.

"I've never heard any Native American stories about Bigfoot. At least I don't think I have," Ben said. "Would you tell me your story? The one that your grandfather told you?"

"Sure I will. I'm a Yakama Indian," Jim explained. "I grew up on the reservation near Yakima, Washington. In my grandfather's legend, Bigfoot is called *Ste-ye-hah'*. That means 'spirit hiding under the cover of the woods.'

"Our legends say that there are many of these spirits. The plural is *Ste-ye-hah'-mah*. But I'll just use *Stick Shower Indians*. That's what we call them in English."

Jim and Ben sat on the back porch. Jim told the story. And Ben blocked out the rest of the world. Jim's deep voice was the only thing he heard.

Long, long ago, there was a strong Yakama Indian. His name was Two Feathers. And he was a great hunter.

Now legend has it that the wild Stick Shower Indians roamed

the forests of the Cascades. Two Feathers had never seen one. And he had no idea that he was about to.

Two Feathers was resting in his tepee. He kept hearing a strange birdcall. But he couldn't place it.

He was very tired. He'd had a long day of hunting. So he stoked the fire outside. And he settled into the tepee for the night.

A few minutes later, he heard a rustling sound outside. It didn't worry him. For he knew that he shared the land with other creatures.

Then the warm summer breeze blew in a strong, foul odor. Two Feathers could barely breathe! He covered his mouth and nose with a blanket.

It will pass, he thought.

Suddenly, a giant arm thrust through the tepee's opening! It was black and hairy. And it was waving a stick!

Two Feathers was alarmed. "Who's there?" he asked.

Slowly, he reached for his bow and arrow. He turned his back to the opening for just a moment. And he was showered with hundreds of sticks.

He wasn't hurt. But he was confused. "Show yourself!" he demanded.

Cautiously, he crept outside. His fire had been stomped out. And an apelike creature was running away. The creature was wearing the head of a bear. Two Feathers had never seen anything like it.

Now the moonlight was clear and bright. But it was not bright enough for Two Feathers to chase after the beast. It would be too dark in the **dense** woods. Not to mention that he couldn't run after the creature alone. For what might he find?

Instead, Two Feathers built a new fire. And he kept watch all night. The animal never returned.

At first sun, he followed the beast's tracks into the woods. But after a hundred yards or so, they disappeared. No more tracks! No sign of the Stick Shower Indian!

Two Feathers returned to his tribe. And he told his tale. An **elder** said, "Ah! Stick Shower sightings are very rare! Very rare, indeed."

The elder said that Stick Showers lived in underground lodges. The doors were protected under earth and snow. He said that no man could find the doors.

Two Feathers mentioned the head of the bear. The elder explained that a Stick Shower wore a bearskin. It kept him warm. He tied it over himself with strings.

"As for the disappearing footprints," said the elder, "the Stick Showers grow magical berries. They use them to make a special **elixir.** The potion makes them swifter than the wind. They can become invisible if necessary."

The elder also explained that Stick Showers were expert hunters. And they didn't like to share. So there would be trouble if a man hunted where a Stick Shower wanted to hunt.

It seems that Two Feathers had been lucky. The "shower of sticks" was a warning from the Stick Shower Indian. He was telling Two Feathers to move on. To leave his territory.

If Two Feathers hadn't left, there might have been real trouble. The Stick Shower might have pushed him off a cliff. Or drowned him in the river. He could have done so without leaving a clue. And it would have looked like an accident.

And that is why the Yakama Indians respect the Stick Shower Indians. And they try to **coexist** with the spirits in peace.

Jim finished his tale.

"I love that!" Ben remarked. "Your story is so different from the ones I've heard." He paused, then added, "Yet it's still the same in some ways."

"Exactly!" exclaimed Jim. "There are too many Bigfoot legends to count. In some he's a spirit. Or a ghost. In others he's some type of gorilla.

"He's been called a form of primitive man. Some say that the creature is always female. And, as you heard, the Yakamas tell of a wild tribe of American Indians."

"I think I'd better go back to camp now," Ben said. "Say hi to Mr. Cooper for me."

"Do you want me to tell him that I spilled the beans?"

"It's up to you. I'm not mad about it," Ben replied. "He did make this trip memorable for me. And I had fun talking to him."

"Maybe you ought to tell him that," said Jim.

"I will," Ben said. "I'll let him know. Thanks for all the great information." He dangled his grocery bag in front of him. "And thanks for this."

Ben walked slowly back to camp. He had a lot to think about.

Examples of Bigfoot Folklore

Chinese

The Chinese Wildman is well over six feet tall. It has grayish red fur. And it can run very fast. It is very strong. And it has huge teeth shaped like a human's.

Hoopa

The Hoopa Indians of northern California refer to Sasquatch as "boss of the mountains." He takes care of the mountains. But he has no interest in the people.

Karok

According to a Karok legend of long ago, Bigfoot-like creatures lived in the mountains. They were called *Upslope Persons*. And they were big, strong, stupid, and hairy. They were to be feared. And it was said that they captured and ate children!

Examples of Bigfoot Folklore (continued)

Mohawk

In Mohawk Indian folklore, Bigfoot is a spirit. He can appear and disappear whenever he wants to. If someone shoots him, he will not fall down. He will choose to disappear into thin air. And he will go heal his wounds.

Salish

The Salish Indian tribe of British Columbia call Bigfoot *Sasquatch*. The Salish believe Sasquatch is a wild man who forever lives in the woods.

Sherpa

The Sherpa of Nepal believe that Yeti **patrols** the snowy mountains. He is said to be up to 15 feet tall.

Yurok

Legend has it that one young woman met four giants who lived on the ridge. She married one. And she had his baby. People telling the story today refer to her giant husband as Bigfoot.

Meanwhile, Mr. Cooper pulled up to the store. He honked when he saw Jim.

"I had to pick up a few things," he called out. "Have you been waiting long?"

"No—not long," Jim smiled. "You just missed a customer, though."

"That's too bad. Hope he comes back."

"I went ahead and helped him," Jim added merrily. "But I have a feeling he'll be back."

Chapter 7

A Vacation to Remember

The Davises explored the area for a couple more days. Ben thought a lot about Mr. Cooper, Jim—and Bigfoot.

Ben still didn't quite know what to believe. Part of him wanted to dismiss Bigfoot. To view him—or it—as a character in lots of great stories. But another part of him wanted to think that Bigfoot might be out there.

Ben knew that intelligent people were studying the possibility. He'd keep an open mind and see if anyone came up with definite information either way. He knew there were lots of investigators. And lots of reporters too. Someday, everyone would know for sure.

An Interview with Reporter Greg Long

Here's an interview with a real-life Bigfoot reporter. Greg Long works as a technical writer and editor. In his spare time, he writes detailed articles about current Bigfoot sightings and investigations. These reports appear on his Web site. It's called Northwest Mysteries: Exploration into the Unknown. You can find it at http://www.nwmyst.com/nwmyst-bigfoot.html. Check it out! You'll find articles on all kinds of mysteries. And there are lots of colorful photos too.

Question: How did you become interested in reporting on Bigfoot?

Answer: While looking into [a story] on the Yakama Indian Reservation, I became interested in Bigfoot reports. I interviewed several people on the reservation regarding Bigfoot.

Question: What kind of response do you get from your readers?

Answer: I get a very positive response. Readers want more information on the subject.

Question: Briefly, what is the most interesting Bigfoot-related story you've ever investigated?

Answer: Todd Neiss's sighting is the most interesting. As a witness, Neiss is excellent. He had little or no interest in Bigfoot before his sighting. In short, Neiss saw three large Bigfoot creatures. This happened while he was handling explosive charges during Army National Guard training in northwestern Oregon. (Note: The full story can be found on Mr. Long's Web site.)

Question: Have you ever had a Bigfoot sighting?

Answer: No sighting. Anything is possible. To see Bigfoot, I need to locate those areas with a greater than even chance of potential Bigfoot presence. I am always hopeful that I will see Bigfoot.

Question: Have you ever been given tips that were clearly hoaxes?

Answer: No—none that were hoaxes.

Question: Do you think that the issue of whether Bigfoot exists will ever be settled?

Answer: I believe the issue will be resolved. But likely not in my lifetime. Proper funding and [scientific research] have not been adequately brought to bear on the subject. Until that happens, **amateur** investigation will [be common] in the field.

Question: What advice would you give to kids who want to learn more about Bigfoot?

Answer: Children are more open-minded to the possibilities of mysteries such as Bigfoot, and so forth. Children need to read as much as they can on Bigfoot. They can go to their local library. They may even be able to go on a search for Bigfoot under adult supervision. This means attending meetings held by Bigfoot investigators. And they could accompany Bigfoot investigators on interviews and field trips. Nothing substitutes for old-fashioned detective work!

Then again, Ben thought, I do want to have fun with this. Like Mr. Cooper.

Jim had been right. Mr. Cooper's fun really contributed to the Bigfoot myth. It was fun to wonder about it. And it was fun to be scared about it.

My friends will just die over my stories, Ben thought. He couldn't wait to show them his pictures! Then they could make up their own minds too.

Finally, the Davises were packed and ready to drive home. They stopped at the Trading Post.

"Okay, kids," said Jack. "You know the drill. I'm going to fill up the gas tank. You go in and get us all some drinks for the road."

"What's Mom going to do?" Jess asked.

Brooke answered as she stepped out of the minivan. "I'm going to enjoy the mountain air. For just a little while longer!"

Mr. Cooper greeted Ben and Jess warmly. "Hello. Are you leaving today?"

"Yes," said Jess. "We should be home later tonight. Dad's filling up. And we need to get some sodas."

"Well, I'm glad you stopped in," said Mr. Cooper.

"Jess?" Ben asked. "Grab a root beer for me. And get one of those flavored teas for Dad. And a big bottle of water for Mom."

"Okay," Jess said. She wandered to the refrigerated case to make her selections.

"How was the Golden Gate Trail?" Mr. Cooper asked, smiling slyly. "See anything interesting?"

"I sure did," Ben answered with a grin. "I have quite a story to tell my friends."

"Glad to hear it!" Mr. Cooper exclaimed.

"I'll never forget this vacation, Mr. Cooper. And I'll never forget you."

Just then, Brooke and Jack walked in.

"Hi, Sam," said Brooke. "Thanks for spending time with Ben. He really enjoyed himself. Right, Ben?"

"Definitely," Ben replied.

"I assure you, ma'am, that it was my pleasure," beamed Mr. Cooper.

"By the way, Ben," Brooke added. "You never told me. Did Mr. Cooper make a Bigfoot believer out of you?"

Ben looked at Mr. Cooper. And he gave him a big wink. Then he turned to Brooke.

"Well, Mom," he said. "I'm afraid that's strictly between me—and me!"

The Big Question

The question remains: Does Bigfoot exist? To this day, there is no proof—one way or the other! No one has been able to offer definite proof that he doesn't exist. Yet no one has ever captured a convincing specimen.

Ben decided to keep an open mind. And to add to the legend surrounding Bigfoot.

What about you? If you don't believe in Bigfoot, what would it take to change your mind? And if you do believe in Bigfoot, what evidence convinced you?

Regardless of your beliefs, you must admit that the riddle of Bigfoot's existence is fun to think about. People continue to claim to see him. Scholars continue to study the possibility. Adventurers still try to track him. And for countless reasons, the legend of Bigfoot lives on.

Glossary

amateur	nonprofessional
artifact	something created by humans for a specific purpose—it remains from a previous era
authenticity	genuineness
climate	the average weather conditions at a place
coexist	to live, or exist, together
credibility	the quality or power of creating belief
data	factual information
dense	thick with leaves
elder	one having authority because he or she is older and has more experience
elevation	the height above the level of the sea
elixir	a potion
fauna	the animals that are typically found in a given region or environment
flora	the plants that are typically found in a given region or environment
Gigantopithecus	an enormous ape that existed in the Pliocene and Pleistocene eras
gullible	especially trusting
haven	a place of safety

hoax	a prank or practical joke
inhabit	to live in a place
legend	a story that is passed down from generation to generation
memorabilia	mementos; items that stir memories
offensive	sickening; disgusting
oral tradition	the practice of telling stories that explain a culture's beliefs and history
patrol	to watch or to guard
perspective	point of view
produce	fresh fruits and vegetables
specimen	example
subalpine	related to growing on high mountain slopes
tabloid	newspaper that typically features exaggerated stories

References

Books

Byrne, Peter. *The Search for Bigfoot: Monster, Myth, or Man?*, Pocket Books, New York, 1976.

Gaffron, Norma. *Bigfoot,* Greenhaven Press, San Diego, 1989.

Pyle, Robert Michael. *Where Bigfoot Walks: Crossing the Dark Divide,* Houghton Mifflin, New York, 1995.

Krantz, Grover. *Big Footprints: A Scientific Inquiry into the Reality of Sasquatch,* Johnson Books, Boulder, CO, 1992.

Patterson, Roger. *Do Abominable Snowmen Really Exist?*, Franklin Press, Yakima, WA, 1966.

Stein, Gordon, and Marie J. MacNee. *Hoaxes! Dupes, Dodges & Other Dastardly Deceptions,* Visible Ink Press, Detroit, 1995.

Documentaries

Ancient Mysteries: Bigfoot for A&E, 1994.

The Quest: Bigfoot for The Learning Channel, 1996.

Web Sites

Links to Bigfoot Web sites
http://www.teleport.com/"biggie/fglinks.html

Mount Rainier National Park
http://www.nps.gov/mora/home.htm

Northwest Mysteries: Exploration into the Unknown
http://www.nwmyst.com/nwmyst-bigfoot.html

ParkNet: The National Park Service
http://www.nps.gov/

Yakama Nation Cultural Center
http://www.tricity.wsu.edu/~pkeller/tc/museums/Yakama-center.html

Index